D1107236

Over
in the
Meadow

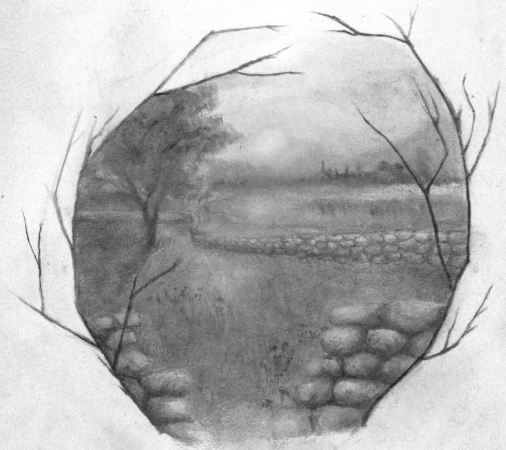

Adapted by
John M. Feierabend

Illustrated by
Marissa Napoletano

G-9032
ISBN: 978-1-62277-178-3
This book was printed in December 2015 by RR Donnelley in Shenzhen, China.

Over in the meadow, in the sand in the sun,
Lived an old mother turtle and her little turtle one.
"Dig," said the mother, "I dig," said the one.
So he dug and was glad in the sand in the sun.

Over in the meadow where the tall grasses grew,
Lived an old mother fox and her little foxes two.
"Run," said the mother. "We run," said the two;
So they ran and were glad where the tall grasses grew.

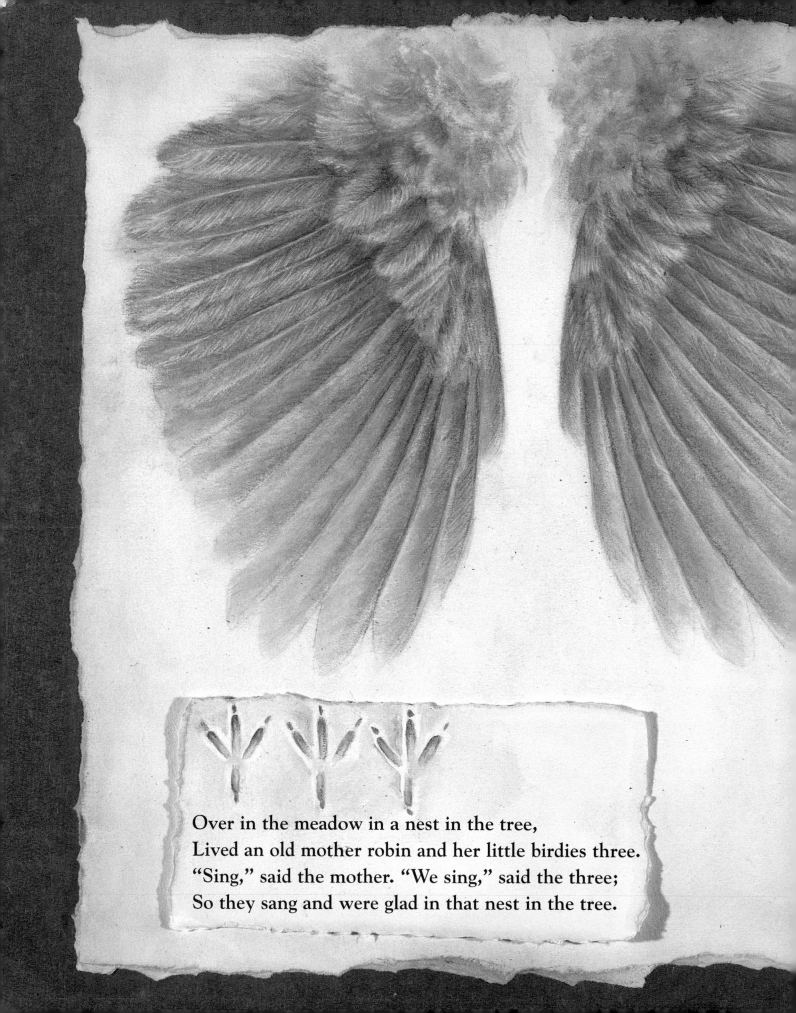

Over in the meadow in a nest in the tree,
Lived an old mother robin and her little birdies three.
"Sing," said the mother. "We sing," said the three;
So they sang and were glad in that nest in the tree.

Over in the meadow in a tall sycamore,
Lived an old mother chipmunk and her little chipmunks four.
"Play," said the mother. "We play," said the four;
So they played and were glad in that tall sycamore.

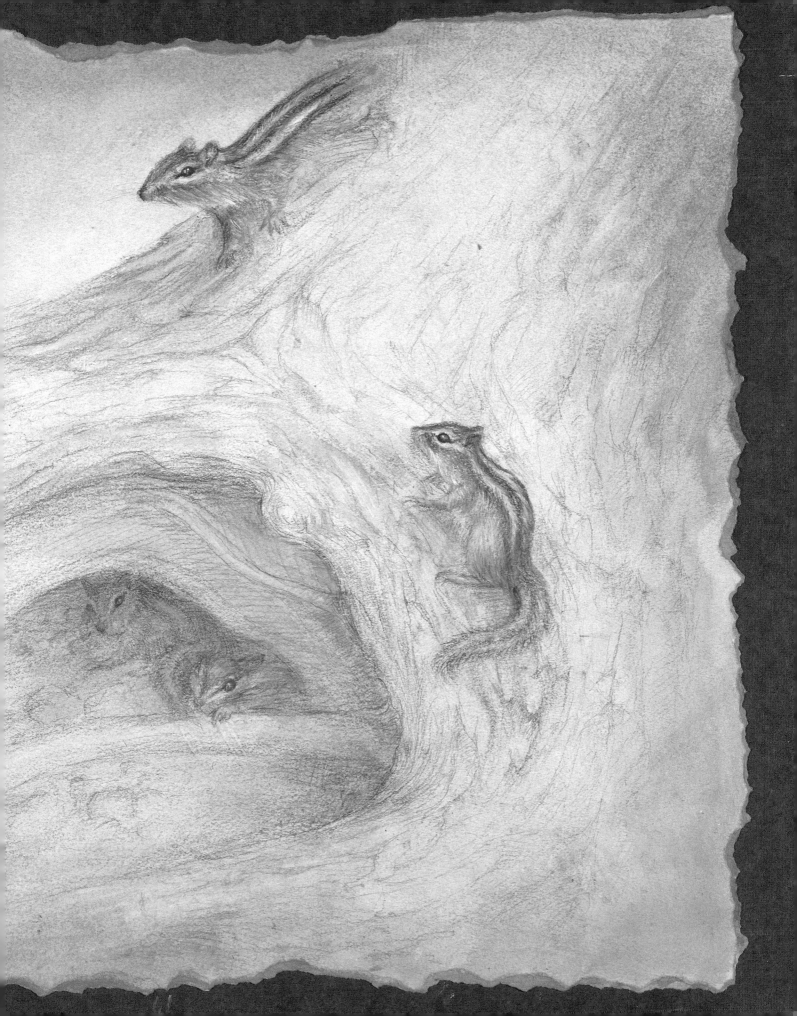

Over in the meadow in a new little hive,
Lived an old mother bee and her honeybees five.
"Bzzz," said the mother. "We bzzz," said the five;
So they bzzzed and were glad in their new little hive.

Over in the meadow in a dam built of sticks,
Lived an old mother beaver and her little beavers six.
"Build," said the mother. "We build," said the six;
So they built and were glad in the dam built of sticks.

Over in the meadow in the green wet bogs,
Lived an old mother froggie and her seven polliwogs.

"Swim," said the mother.
"We swim," said the 'wogs;

So they swam and were glad
in the green wet bogs.

Over in the meadow as the day grew late,
Lived an old mother owl and her little owls eight.

"Wink," said the mother.
"We wink," said the eight;

So they winked and were glad
as the day grew late.

Over in the meadow in a web on the pine,
Lived an old mother spider and her little spiders nine.

"Spin," said the mother.
"We spin," said the nine;

So they spun and were glad
in their web on the pine.

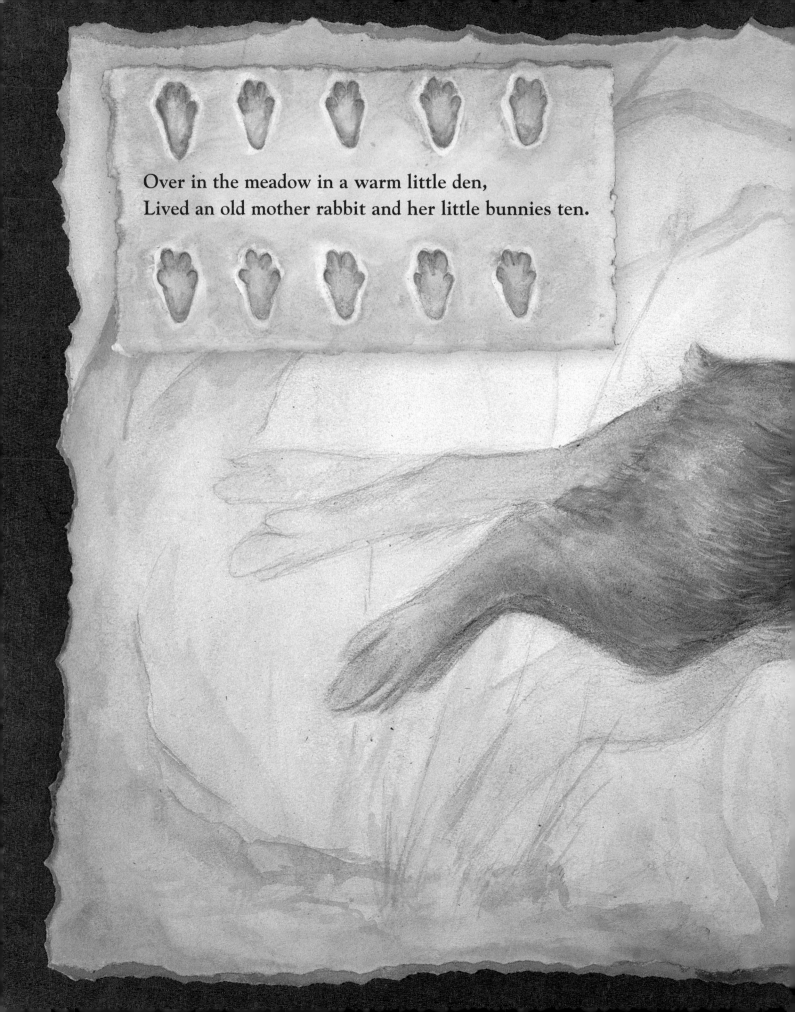

Over in the meadow in a warm little den,
Lived an old mother rabbit and her little bunnies ten.

"Hop," said the mother.
"We hop," said the ten;

So they hopped and were glad in their warm little den.

Over
in the
Meadow

O-ver in the mead-ow, in the sand in the sun, Lived an

old moth-er tur-tle and her lit-tle tur-tle one.

"Dig," said the moth-er, "I dig," said the one. So he

dug and was glad in the sand in the sun.

For a free mp3 version of this song, visit giamusic.com/meadow

2. Over in the meadow where the tall grasses grew,
   Lived an old mother fox and her little foxes two.
   "Run," said the mother. "We run," said the two;
   So they ran and were glad where the tall grasses grew.

3. Over in the meadow in a nest in the tree,
   Lived an old mother robin and her little birdies three.
   "Sing," said the mother. "We sing," said the three;
   So they sang and were glad in that nest in the tree.

4. Over in the meadow in a tall sycamore,
   Lived an old mother chipmunk and her little
      chipmunks four.
   "Play," said the mother. "We play," said the four;
   So they played and were glad in that tall sycamore.

5. Over in the meadow in a new little hive,
   Lived an old mother bee and her honeybees five.
   "Bzzz," said the mother. "We bzzz," said the five;
   So they bzzzed and were glad in their new little hive.

6. Over in the meadow in a dam built of sticks,
   Lived an old mother beaver and her little beavers six.
   "Build," said the mother. "We build," said the six;
   So they built and were glad in the dam built of sticks.

7. Over in the meadow in the green wet bogs,
   Lived an old mother froggie and her seven polliwogs.
   "Swim," said the mother. "We swim," said the 'wogs;
   So they swam and were glad in the green wet bogs.

8. Over in the meadow as the day grew late,
   Lived an old mother owl and her little owls eight.
   "Wink," said the mother. "We wink," said the eight;
   So they winked and were glad as the day grew late.

9. Over in the meadow in a web on the pine,
   Lived an old mother spider and her little spiders nine.
   "Spin," said the mother. "We spin," said the nine;
   So they spun and were glad in their web on the pine.

10. Over in the meadow in a warm little den,
    Lived an old mother rabbit and her little bunnies ten.
    "Hop," said the mother. "We hop," said the ten;
    So they hopped and were glad in their warm little den.

About Over in the Meadow

Over in the meadow... there lives a wonderful array of animals and their young. This traditional folksong probably originated in the United Kingdom in the sixteenth century and then spread to other countries. In the Ozarks in 1882, Katherine Floyd Dana (under the pen name Olive A. Wadsworth) wrote down the words, and Mabel Wood Hill notated the music to be preserved for generations to sing. Cecil Sharp later collected "Over in the Meadow" and published it in his 1917 collection *English Folk Songs from the Southern Appalachians*.

"Over in the Meadow" has not only served many generations as a song to teach counting and rhyming. It is also a delightful introduction to the wonderful natural world that we share with our animal friends.

Through the years Wadsworth's collection of meadow dwellers has seen many changes. Her version begins the tale with "an old mother toadie and her little toadie one, who wink to each other in the sand and the sun," but other words for the song begin with a horse by a stream or a duck in a pond. The many contributions and adaptations to the song by others gives evidence that the song has been widely popular.

In addition to the lyrics that are included in this book, here are some of the animals that make appearances in other versions of the song.

Continued on next page

One

A lovely brown horse and her little baby one, who
    "neighs" by the stream in the sun
An old mother duck and her little duck one, who
    "quacks" in a pond in the sun
An old mother frog and her little froggy one, who
    "croaks" by the big shady tree
An old mother frog and her little froggy one, who hop
    in a pond in the sun

Two

An old mother fish and her little fishes two, who swim
    in a stream so blue
An old mother sheep and her little lambs two, who
    "baa" where the streams run through
An old mother fish and her little fishes two, who swim
    in the stream so blue
An old mother cat and her little kittens two, who
    "purr" in a worn out shoe
An old daddy red fox and his little foxes two, who run
    where the tall grass grew
A woolly mother sheep and her little lambies two,
    who "baa" where the sky gleams blue

Three

An old mother bluebird and her little birdies three,
    who sing in a hole in the tree
An old mother owl and her little owls three, who
    "whoo" in a hole in the tree
An old mother frog and her little froggies three, who
    "croak" by the pond near the tree
An old mother bird and her little birdies three, who
    sing on the branch of a tree
A spotted mother cow and her spotted babies three,
    who "moo" by the big shady tree

Four

An old mother frog and her little frogs four, who "rib-
    bit" on a rock by the shore
An old mother duck and her little ducks four, who
    "quack" away from the shore
An old mother rat and her little ratties four, who gnaw
    by the old barn door
An old mother muskrat and her little ratties four, who
    dive in the reeds by the shore
An old mother worm and her little wormies four, who
    squirm in an old apple core

Five

An old mother bee and her little bees five, who "buzz"
    in a snug beehive
An old mother butterfly and her group of five, who flap
    by the big beehive

Six

A black mother crow and her little crows six, who
    "caw" in a nest built of sticks
An old mother dog and her little puppies six, who
    "bark" in a house made of sticks

Seven

An old mother frog and her little froggies seven, who
    jump where the grass grows so even
A gay mother cricket and her little crickets seven, who
    "chirp" where the grass is so even
An old mother owl and her owlets seven, who "hoot"
    in the tree of heaven
A furry mother mouse and her little mousies seven,
    who "squeak" where the grass is so even

Eight

A brown mother lizard and her little lizards eight, who
    bask by the old mossy gate
An old mother duck and her little ducklings eight, who
    "quack" in an old packing crate

Nine

An old mother duck and her little duckies nine, who
    "quack" by the old scotch pine
A green mother frog and her little froggies nine, who
    "croak" where the quiet pools shine
An old mother mouse and her little mice nine, who
    "squeak" on a ball of twine
A slippery mother fish and her little fishes nine, who
    swim where the stream water shines

Ten

An old mother beaver and her little beavers ten, who
    beave in a cozy wee den
A gray mother spider and her little spiders ten, who
    spin in a sly little den

Now, it's your turn to join in as so many others have done before. Enjoy the pleasure of creating new verses about the creatures who live and thrive in your own favorite meadow!